10-200
COME ON,
SMOKEY!

10-200 COME ON, SMOKEY!

By Bob Cunningham

Illustrations by Rod and Barbara Furan

Library of Congress Catalog Card Number: 76-051142. International Standard Book Number: 0-913940-55-0.

The big old CB Jamboree was on!

Neil Hawkins drove his 4-wheeler into the State Park. The speaker of his two-way crackled out the news.

"Hey, good buddy, put the pedal to the metal and scratch on over to Kiona River Park. The whole wide CB world is here today for the Jamboree. We gonna have a bodacious time!"

"Breaker One-Four for that Buffalo Chip. You gotta copy on this Snaggletooth? We need a radio check on this new power mike, come on."

"I gotcha, Snaggletooth. Mercy sakes, you're comin' in wall-to-wall and treetop tall. You better buy that thing. You never been so easy to pull out!"

"Break Channel Seven. How about the Goldenrod? Goldie, did our little rug rats sneak over to your camper? We can't eyeball 'em anywhere."

"What about that Tater Trap one time, we listenin', KTG-5247, Running Bear."

"Breakity-break Two-Oh for a radio check. Any good buddy gotta copy on this weakie mo-byle, what say?"

"How about it, Pill Roller, we need you at the first-aid 20. Spaghetti Betty, WATCH Unit 3, KFK-4236 by."

TO THE READER: ALL CB TERMS ARE EXPLAINED IN THE GLOSS-ARY ON PAGES 30-31.

Neil's 4-wheel drive Scout joined a parade of vehicles that were rolling toward the main picnic grounds. All of the cars and campers and pickups bristled with antennas. Many of the drivers were happily talking into microphones. It looked like all the CB-radio fans in Cascade City were gathering for the Jamboree.

The picnic grounds looked like a carnival.

CB clubs from all over Oregon and Washington were there with signs and banners. Club members, wearing colored vests, went around trading club shoulder patches and QSL cards.

Children with toy radios played walkie-talkie hide and seek. Loudspeakers announced ratchet-jaw contests and demonstrations of new radios and antennas. Tables were covered with CB gear that people wanted to trade or sell.

Bar-B-Q pits smoked. Vats of sweet corn steamed. People ate and talked and played games and had a fine time.

Neil Hawkins was the outdoor editor for the Cascade City Journal. Most of the time, he wrote newspaper stories about hunting, fishing, and camping. Today he was going to do a different kind of article. He was going to write about his hobby, CB radio.

There was no better place to do it than a CB Jamboree!

It was a picnic and swap-meet and a gab fest and a camp-out all rolled into one. Neil's children, Ryan and Kristi, had come along to join the fun. Neil's wife, Sara, who was a photographer, had come to take pictures of the Jamboree.

Neil said, "Let's all put on labels with our handles. Everybody's wearing them."

The Hawkins' each got a tag with his CB-land name written on it. Neil was Sky Hawk. Sara was Pigeon Hawk. Kristi and Ryan were Day Hawk and Night Hawk.

You don't have to have a CB handle. Your FCC official license contains only letters and numbers, but handles were part of the fun of CB radios. One of the most amusing things about a Jamboree was matching handles with the people who wore them. For example, if you had never seen your CB friend Hot Lips, you might be surprised to find she's a gray-haired grandmother!

The Hawkins children went off to watch the games. Neil and Sara wandered through the display area, making notes and taking photos.

They saw CB radios built into sports cars and campers and motorcycles. One proud man showed a wheeled dog-sled with four grinning huskies — fully radio-equipped.

People showed off CB's for bicycles, CB's for boats, CB's for back-packers. A smiling girl had a beautiful saddle on display. Only the antenna sticking out the back showed that it had a built-in CB radio.

A tent under the tall Douglas-firs carried a poster for WATCH. This was the CB group that the Hawkins' belonged to. The volunteers of WATCH monitored Channel 9, the official emergency channel of the Citizens Band. People with problems could call Channel 9 and get help from members of WATCH, REACT, ALERT, or other volunteer public service groups.

Most of the time, Channel 9 monitors helped motorists who were out of gas or lost. There were other times when the volunteers helped with more serious emergencies.

Neil greeted the woman who was in charge of the WATCH tent. "Hi, Betty. We heard you give a shout for Pill Roller as we were driving in. Anything serious?"

"Some turkey shorted his 12-volt and got a little burn. Nothing Doc Baines couldn't fix with his eyes shut."

"Any more of the WATCH gang here?"

"I saw Pink Squirrel and Moon Doggie awhile ago and Granny Peach is helping with the soda pop booth. Let's see . . . Running Bear has his Tijuana taxi sorting out traffic jams somewhere and Midnite Mush-Mouth is over in the display area showing off his fantastic new 4-wheeler with the SSB mobile."

"I'll sit here and ratchet-jaw with Betty," Sara said. "You can check out Mush's new toy."

"Ten-Four, gals. Catch you later," Neil said.

Neil walked off to find his friend Mike Mora, whose handle was Midnite Mush-Mouth. Mush stood guarding the most gaudy 4-wheeler in the display area. It was a brand-new Blazer, scarlet with customized decorations, packed with high priced radio gear.

"She is a sure winner in the Magnificient Mobile contest!" Mush told Neil proudly. "You be sure Sara takes a picture of it for the newspaper."

Suddenly the public address system said: "Break-break-break, folks! Look up in the sky! At this very minute, our good buddy, Captain Courageous, is flyin' over head with his XYL, Angel Eyes. They're gonna sky dive into the Jamboree!"

The crowd cheered and clapped.

"Those sky divers got ears! Go to Channel 6 and you can read 'em as they drop down." The crowd began to run to a nearby field where the parachutists would land.

"C'mon, Hawk," exclaimed Midnite Mush-Mouth. "I gotta catch this!"

Neil and his friend joined the rushing crowd. Meanwhile, a little white airplane circled overhead. People with hand-held CB-units put them to their ears and listened as they ran.

"There they go!" yelled Mush. Two dots fell from the airplane. After a short free fall, striped ribbon-chutes opened like bright mushrooms. The CBers watched in amazement as the sky divers floated downward.

Sara Hawkins came dashing to join her husband. She photographed the sky divers, who steered by tugging their shroud-lines.

"They're gonna land right here!" said Mush.

Hundreds of Jamboree-goers stared upward. Cheers and claps rang out as the sky divers made expert landings on a cloth bullseye. The sky divers showed how CB radio units were entirely self-contained in their helmets.

"I wouldn't have missed that for anything," Mush said with a grin. "Hey, Pigeon Hawk, this ole buffalo of yours said you might take a picture of my new wheels. I'm fixin' to win the Magnificent Mobile contest with it."

"Why, 30-12, Mush," Sara said. "Let's go." They pushed their way through the mob. The display area was nearly deserted because of the sky diving excitement.

"I'm parked right here," Mush said. Then he stopped short and stared at the spot where his beautiful Blazer had stood.

It was gone. The only trace of it was a set of tire tracks in the grass, leading to the road.

"I don't believe this," poor Mush said. "But now that I think of it, I did forget and leave the keys in her and now somebody's ripped her off!"

The PA system sent out a call. "Running Bear, 10-200 at the WATCH tent. All WATCH team members, 10-25 the tent."

A brown and white sheriff's patrol car came bouncing over the grass. Deputy Frank Ralston, alias Running Bear, leaned out of the window. "You gave a shout for the County Mounties?"

Neil said: "Looks like somebody stole Mush's pretty new 4-wheeler. The red Blazer with all the goodies hung on it."

"It would've won the Magnificent Mobile contest!" Mush exclaimed sadly.

The deputy quickly took down the license number and description of the missing car. "I'll send out a bulletin. It can't have gotten far."

The patrol car went off with its bubble gum machine advertising. Neil turned to the WATCHers.

"Good buddies, some road apple has ripped off Midnite Mush-Mouth's new 4-wheeler. Frank's gone off with a 10-200. He'll put the Smokeys on it. I think the rest of us ought to get our own thing going. What say?"

"Ten-Four!" bellowed the gang.

Volunteer emergency groups had a duty to help the authorities but they also had to remember they were not police. Well-meaning amateurs could be pests if they got in the way during emergencies.

"Running Bear will give us a holler on Niner if he spots anything. We'll do the same for him."

Young Ryan Hawkins dashed up with a road map. He gave it to his father. "We'll do a quick search of the park," Neil said. "Here are your assignments . . ."

The CB club members ran to their 4-wheelers. Within seconds, more than a dozen WATCH cars were rolling. Each had a driver and a "shotgun rider," who did most of the eyeballing and kept in radio contact with the rest of the pack.

"Foxy Rebel, Unit Two. Nobody in the campground saw a red Blazer."

"Granny Peach, Unit Nine. He didn't come down by the river."

"Break Channel Niner. This is Running Bear! Subject vehicle reported on highway outside park ten minutes ago. Heading toward the freeway. We'll pedal down and 10-10."

At this news, all the WATCH cars headed for the main road. Neil, whose 4-wheeler was being driven by Mush-Mouth, gave instructions to the others.

"When you get to the Interstate, spread the word on all channels. I'll take One-Seven. Pill-Roller, you monitor Nine and give me a shout if Running Bear comes on with anything hot."

"Ten-Roger," said Dr. Baines.

As Neil's car came close to the freeway, he broke the truckers' channel.

"Break One-Seven for a 10-33. All you gear-jammers on this Big Nickel watch for a new Chevy Blazer, bright red, custom plates M-U-S-H, that's Mush on the tags. This car is stolen and rollin' and it's got ears."

"Ten-Four, guy, we lookin' and cookin'," said a voice.

Neil replied, "Anybody get an eyeball on it, come on back to Sky Hawk, KCW-0484. Or give a holler to the Smokes on Channel Niner. We 10-10."

"Ten-Forty-Roger."

Other WATCH units reported the message had been given on all other CB channels. Then they all monitored 17, where travelers on Interstate 5 did most of their talking. Long minutes passed. Neil repeated his message from time to time and at last he hit paydirt.

"Hey, Sky Hawk, I think I gotta goodie for you. There was a red Blazer northbound. He peeled off at the I-205 bypass. Could be that's your boy, c'mon."

"Ten-Four, rascal, and we thank ya kindly," said Neil. Quickly, he switched to Channel 9. "Break for Running Bear or any other Smokey. We got a 20 on that stolen Blazer, northbound on 205. Sky Hawk, KCW-0484 by."

"Ten-Four, Running Bear by, KTG-5247, and we're putting in the 10-200."

"Sky Hawk 10-27 to One-Seven." Neil switched to the truckers' channel again and gave the word to the WATCH cars. Whatever their location, they now began to head for the I-205 bypass. The stolen car had a good ten minutes' head start. There was an excellent chance the thief was eavesdropping over the CB radio, hearing everything his pursuers said!

Luckily, Neil was in a good pursuit position. Mush drove them onto I-205. They sped through the hills. Neil questioned oncoming drivers who might have seen the stolen car.

"Break for any southbounder on this 205 slab. We got a stolen red Blazer northbound on the boulevard. Anybody get an eyeball on it? Come on back to Sky Hawk, KCW-0484."

"Mercy sakes, guy, we sure did see it," a voice said. "We hauling this load of sticks onto the freeway at Route 212 when a bear-bait Blazer went streaking past going thataway."

"Eastbound on 212, 10-9?"

"Roger-Four for shore," said the log-truck driver. "Heading right into the mountains."

Neil thanked the log-hauler. He went to Channel 9, raised Running Bear, and gave him the revised 20 of the stolen vehicle.

"Ten-Four, Sky Hawk," said the deputy. "Now you keep those WATCH cars safe while we bears put the hammer down. We got two County Mounties, three State Patrol Smokes, a Local Smokel from Clackamette and a Salem bear-in-the-air rung in on this 10-200."

"Come on, ride 'em, Smokey!" yelled Midnite Mush-Mouth.

Neil promised to keep the WATCH volunteers out of the way.

A job the WATCHers could do was to monitor the CB bands. Neil put everyone to work asking mobile CBers for an update on the stolen car's 20.

"This is Italian Stallion, Unit Three. A 4-wheeler saw the Blazer eastbound with fire in its tail ten miles out of Clackamette."

"Moon Doggie here," said a teenage voice. "The subject vehicle seems to have turned off. None of the westbounders coming down the mountain have spotted it."

"Break, you people looking for that red Blazer. This is Abominable Snow-Doll," said a woman. "I think that car just passed us going about eighty on the road to Gravel Lake."

"Thank you, ma'am!" said Neil. He relayed the new 20 to the police. Then he directed Mush to drive to the top of a high ridge nearby.

Keying the mike, Neil tried to raise somebody in the Gravel Lake area. "Has anybody near Gravel Lake got a copy on this one Sky Hawk, c'mon?"

A slow, lazy voice rolled out of the speaker. "Ay-firmatory, good buddy. You got the old Rock-Crusher speakin' at ya."

"Rock-Crusher, we have a stolen red Chevy Blazer rolling your way. You let us know when you get an eyeball on it, okay?"

"Why my land o'goshen mercy me!" drawled the voice. "That Roger Roller Skate is nosin' my 20. You just 10-6 a short-short."

Once again, Neil relayed the information to the Smokeys on Channel 9. Then he had Mush drive toward Gravel Lake. A day-glo sign warned:

SLOW — MEN WORKING

"Where are those bears?" said Mush. "This dude might get away yet."

"Ho, ho, ho!" came Rock-Crusher's voice. "Gotcha!"

A flash of red and blue lights in the mirror warned Mush and Neil to pull over. Three State Police cars and Running Bear's cruiser flashed by. The Smokey chopper went flapping overhead.

Neil and Mush turned a corner, then pulled up short. The radio said: "Don't nobody hurry. This little feller is goin' no where, no how."

Rock-Crusher leaned down from the cab of his radio-equipped asphalt truck. The rest of the road-repair crew and the police stood there grinning. Even the chopper yoyoed up and down.

Rock-Crusher had dumped a load of soft, steaming hot asphalt on the road. The stolen Blazer had run right into it. It was stuck like a fly in molasses.

Running Bear got out his handcuffs. "Not so fast, Frank," said Mush-Mouth. He took a shovel from a chuckling road crewman.

A shabby looking young man sat in the Blazer. "Out of there and start digging, turkey." Mush ordered. "I still might have a chance to win that Magnificent Mobile contest but I'm gonna need a little help from you. Ten-Four?"

"I hate CB radio," said the young man. He began to dig.

ADVERTISING — flashing lights on police car
AFFIRMATORY — yes, affirmative
BEAR — police officer; also SMOKEY BEAR
BEAR-BAIT — vehicle greatly exceeding speed limit
BEAR-IN-THE-AIR — police aircraft
BIG NICKEL — Interstate 5
BODACIOUS — excellent, pleasing, working well, etc.
BOULEVARD — freeway or super highway
BREAK — request for channel use
BREAKER — (1) request for channel use; (2) person who wants to
          transmit
BREAKITY-BREAK — silly variation of BREAK
BUBBLE GUM MACHINE — lights on top of police car
BUFFALO — a man
BY — standing by; waiting for contact
CATCH YOU LATER — common CBer's farewell
CB — Citizens Band
COMING IN — being received via CB radio
COOKING — traveling in vehicle
COPY — (1) message; (2) to hear or listen in
COUNTY MOUNTIE — sheriff's patrol officer
EARS — a CB radio
EYEBALL — (1) to see or look at; (2) to meet
FCC — Federal Communications Commission, government agency
          that regulates and polices all radio operations
FIRE IN ITS TAIL — speeding
FOUR (4)-WHEELER — automobile; any vehicle with four wheels
GEAR-JAMMERS — truck drivers
GOOD BUDDY — common name for CB operator
HAMMER DOWN — accelerating; speeding
HANDLE — name used by CBer for station identification
HOLLER — call for person over CB radio; also SHOUT
HOW ABOUT — invitation to transmit
JAMBOREE — large meeting of CB fans
LOAD OF STICKS — cargo of logs
LOCAL SMOKEL — town or city police; also CITY KITTY
MERCY, MERCY SAKES — exclamation of surprise, dismay, etc.
MOBILE — CB radio in car or truck, or vehicle that is radio-equipped
MO-BYLE — same as MOBILE
MONITOR — (1) one who listens to a certain channel; (2) listening to
          one channel
ONE-FOUR — Channel 14
ONE-SEVEN — Channel 17, truckers' channel in parts of Pacific North-
          west
PEDAL DOWN — accelerate; speed
PEDAL TO THE METAL — accelerate, speed, hurry
PEEL OFF — turn off; leave freeway

POWER MIKE — a legal accessory that increases the strength of CB signal

PULL OUT — to hear a CB station clearly

QSL CARD — postcard, usually decorated, acknowledging two-way radio contact; originally a ham-radio term (QSL-confirmation of communication)

RADIO CHECK — a request for signal-strength check

RASCAL — name for CB operator

RATCHET-JAW — (1) to talk or gossip; (2) CBer who talks too much or hogs channel

ROAD APPLE — a stupid CB operator or other bad guy

ROGER-FOUR FOR SHORE — Ten-Four; yes; affirmative

ROGER ROLLER SKATE — speeding vehicle

RUG RATS — children

SCRATCH — moving fast

SHORT-SHORT — brief time

SHOUT — call for person over CB radio; also HOLLER

SLAB — highway

SMOKEY, SMOKEY BEAR — police, especially state police wearing broad-brimmed hats

SOUTHBOUNDER — vehicle southbound on highway

SSB — single sideband, a special type of CB transmitter

TEN-FORTY-ROGER — Ten-Four; yes; affirmative

TEN-ROGER — Ten-Four; yes; affirmative

10-4 — affirmative; yes; okay; message received

10-6 — busy, stand by

10-9 — repeat message

10-10 — standing by

10-20 — location; also TWENTY

10-22 — report in person (official 10-code usage)

10-27 — move to Channel

10-33 — emergency

10-200 — police needed

THATAWAY — in the opposite direction; THISAWAY — in the same direction

30-12 — three times 10-4; emphatic yes

TIJUANA TAXI — police car

TURKEY — silly or luckless person

12-VOLT — a type of large battery; auto battery

TWENTY — location; short for 10-20

TWO-OH — Channel 20

TWO-WAY — CB radio

WALL-TO-WALL AND TREETOP TALL — transmitting strong signal

WATCH — fictitious group of CB volunteers that monitors Channel 9 for emergency calls. Initials stand for "Western Auxiliary Team of CB Helpers."

WHAT ABOUT — call for certain CB operator

WHEELS — any vehicle

XYL — wife; literally "ex-young lady," a ham radio term adopted by CBers

"LOOK FOR THE 10-20 OF OUR OTHER NEIL HAWKINS CB ADVENTURES"

10-5 ALASKA SKIP

10-7 FOR GOOD SAM

10-33 EMERGENCY

10-70 RANGE FIRE

CRESTWOOD HOUSE

"KEEP READING."
IT'S A BIG 10-4 FOR YOU.